The Day of the Rainbow

*For Mike Craft with love
from Ruth Craft*

*For Jude Daly with love
from Niki Daly*

VIKING KESTREL

Viking Penguin Inc., 40 West 23rd Street, New York, New York 10010, U.S.A.

First published in Great Britain by William Heinemann Ltd., 1988

First American Edition

Published in 1989

Text copyright © Ruth Craft, 1988

Illustrations copyright © Niki Daly, 1988

Library of Congress catalog card number: 88-50659

ISBN 0-670-82456-9

Printed in Hong Kong by Mandarin Offset

The Day of the Rainbow

WRITTEN BY RUTH CRAFT · ILLUSTRATED BY NIKI DALY

VIKING KESTREL

Hot and cross
in the summer sun,
as cross as the shoppers
when the buses won't run,
hot and cross
in the summer sun
lies the big city.

Here trails Nerinder,
not really trying
to keep up
with that lot.
It's too hot.

Mom's cross,
and the new baby too.
And the old baby
kicks up
one huge great
steaming
hullabaloo!

Shopping goes
flopping!
Library books
flap-smack-dropping!
Eggs slopping,
slipitty-slop.

And in all the gefuffle,
Mike Mulligan
and his loyal steam shovel
e lost
n the gravel
nd papery dust.

Hot and cross
in the summer sun,
as hot as the rollers
in Michelle's salon,
hot and cross
in the summer sun
lies the big city.

Here rolls Leroy
through stuck–fast talkers,
hot walkers,
pavement chalkers.

Like a jiving grasshopper,
he rocks and rolls through
the hot cross shoppers.

Oh!
See that soft package,
wrapped small
as a hamster's ear?

Inside are two earrings,
peacock and shiny blue,

Leroy's lost present
for pretty Lou.

Hot and cross
in the summer sun,
as cross as hot cats
when the dogs
spoil the fun,
hot and cross
in the summer sun
lies the big city.

And in all the fuss,
Chef Dimitri Poppodopolous
is loading
Mrs Eleni Poppodopolous
onto a bus.

She hangs on to her hat,
her black basket,
and Mr Poppodopolous
gets two big kisses,
but Eleni just misses
the one thing she *must* take.
Chef Dimitri's precious recipe
for his rare specialty –
raisin cake.

Look! See!
As the bus whooshes by,
Dimitri's precious recipe
sails high, high, high.
High as the tower blocks
in the hot blue sky.

Hot and cross
in the summer sun,
cross as the buskers
when the customers run,
hot and cross
in the summer sun
lies the big city.

Oh, Nerinder!
A cool cotton lap
while the babies nap,
but no long look
at the new library book.

Oh, Leroy!
What a pickle and stew!
Will a bunch of flowers
have to do?
But that's not good enough
for pretty Lou.

Dimitri Poppodopolous
cross and obstreperous,
crashes the plates!
"Oh, Eleni Poppodopolous!
Silly Eleni Poppodopolous!
For heaven's sake!
How *could* you lose the recipe
for my rare specialty,
my *only* specialty,
raisin cake!"

Now clouds
like grey eiderdowns
wrap over
the hot cross city.

And the rain comes down.

Between towers
of clouds,
a blue space
makes a cool place.

A swerve of red,
orange, yellow, green,
blue, indigo
and violet
makes first a wobbly curve
and now
a rainbow.

It bends and falls
to that magic place
where folks sometimes find
things lost,
things precious,
things left behind.

"Look!"
"Look there in the sky!"
"I might find my book.
  Please let's go and try."

"Perhaps. Maybe.
  We'll just go and see."

On the way,
Nerinder spies
a scrap of blue paper.
The strange spiky writing
catches her eye.

Leroy rolls slowly.
A little curve,
a gentle bend,
rolling towards
the rainbow's end,
for it might just be
that the story is true,
he might find the earrings
for pretty Lou.

But . . . whoops!

What's this?
What's that?
A book's knocked him flat!

Eleni Poppodopolous
thinks all this fuss
about rainbows
is simply ridiculous.
But you never know,
so off she goes
through the cool, damp city
in search of Dimitri's
precious recipe.

Ah-tishoo! Ah-tishoo!
Eleni Poppodopolous
takes out her hanky
and blows her nose.
And there at her feet
is a neat package
of soft white tissue.
Ah-tishoo!
Ah-tishoo!

Ah!
Each finds the other
in the magic place.
Each treasure
goes back
to its own right place,
there's a huge smile
on every face.

Cool and cheerful
in the evening sun
lies the big city.
Cool and cheerful
as hot cross trouble
when it's over
and finished
and settled
and done.